The Wise Man stroked his beard.

"My son," he said, "the matter is simple. True love takes no account of looks."

"No?" said Agravaine.

"You two are affinities. Therefore, to you the outward aspect is nothing. Put it like this. Love is a thingummybob who what-d'you-call-its."

"I'm beginning to see," said Agravaine.

"What I meant was this. Love is a wizard greater than Merlin. He plays odd tricks with the eyesight."

"Yes," said Agravaine.

"Or, put it another way. Love is a sculptor greater than Praxiteles. He takes an unsightly piece of clay and moulds it into a thing divine."

"I get you," said Agravaine.

The Wise Man began to warm to his work.

"Or shall we say——?"

"I think I must be going," said Agravaine. "I promised my wife I would be back early."

"We might put it——" began the Wise Man perseveringly.

"I understand," said Agravaine, hurriedly. "I quite see now. Good-bye."

The Wise Man sighed resignedly.

"Good-bye, Sir Knight," he said. "Good-bye. Pay at ye desk."

And Agravaine rode on his way marvelling.

They looked at each other in the starlight. She held out her hands.

"Agravaine!"

She drooped towards him, and he gathered her into his arms. For a novice, he did it uncommonly well.

It was about six months later that Agravaine, having ridden into the forest, called upon a Wise Man at his cell.

In those days almost anyone who was not a perfect bonehead could set up as a Wise Man and get away with it. All you had to do was to live in a forest and grow a white beard. This particular Wise Man, for a wonder, had a certain amount of rude sagacity. He listened carefully to what the knight had to say.

"It has puzzled me to such an extent," said Agravaine, "that I felt that I must consult a specialist. You see me. Take a good look at me. What do you think of my personal appearance? You needn't hesitate. It's worse than that. I am the ugliest man in England."

"Would you go so far as that?" said the Wise Man, politely.

"Farther. And everybody else thinks so. Everybody except my wife. She tells me that I am a model of manly beauty. You know Lancelot? Well, she said I have Lancelot whipped to a custard. What do you make of that? And here's another thing. It is perfectly obvious to me that my wife is one of the most beautiful creatures in existence. I have seen them all, and I tell you that she stands alone. She is literally marooned in Class A, all by herself. Yet she insists that she is plain. What do you make of it?"

Agravaine nodded. He began to see daylight.

"My sister Yseult was very beautiful. After the first day Sir Sagramore forgot all about the giant, and seemed to want to do nothing else except have Yseult show him how to play cat's cradle. They were married two months later, and my father sent my sister Elaine to Camelot to ask for a knight to protect us against a wild unicorn."

"And who bit?" asked Agravaine, deeply interested.

"Sir Malibran of Devon. They were married within three weeks, and my father—I can't go on. You understand now."

"I understand the main idea," said Agravaine. "But in my case——"

"You were to marry me," said Yvonne. Her voice was quiet and cold, but she was quivering.

Agravaine was conscious of a dull, heavy weight pressing on his heart. He had known his love was hopeless, but even hopelessness is the better for being indefinite. He understood now.

"And you naturally want to get rid of me before it can happen," he said. "I don't wonder. I'm not vain. . . . Well, I'll go. I knew I had no chance. Good-bye."

He turned. She stopped him with a sharp cry.

"What do you mean? You cannot wish to stay now? I am saving you."

"Saving me! I have loved you since the moment you entered the Hall at Camelot," said Agravaine.

She drew in her breath.

"You—you love *me!*"

affairs. After his sojourn in the guarded room, freedom looked very good to him. But freedom meant parting from Yvonne.

He looked at the sky and he looked at the castle walls, and he took a step back towards the door.

"I'm not so sure I want to go," he said.

"Oh, fly! Fly, Sir Knight!" she cried.

"You don't understand," said Agravaine. "I don't want to seem to be saying anything that might be interpreted as in the least derogatory to your father in any way whatever, but without prejudice, surely he is just a plain, ordinary brigand? I mean it's only a question of a ransom? And I don't in the least object——"

"No, no, no." Her voice trembled. "He would ask no ransom."

"Don't tell me he kidnaps people just as a hobby!"

"You don't understand. He—No, I cannot tell you. Fly!"

"What don't I understand?"

She was silent. Then she began to speak rapidly. "Very well. I will tell you. Listen. My father had six children, all daughters. We were poor. We had to stay buried in this out-of-the-way spot. We saw no one. It seemed impossible that any of us should ever marry. My father was in despair. Then he said, 'If we cannot get to town, the town must come to us.' So he sent my sister Yseult to Camelot to ask the king to let us have a knight to protect us against a giant with three heads. There was no giant, but she got the knight. It was Sir Sagramore. Perhaps you knew him?"

And then with amazement he heard the bolt shoot back and a key grate in the keyhole.

The door swung open. It was dark outside, but Agravaine could distinguish a female form, and, beyond, a shapeless mass which he took correctly to be the remains of the two plug-uglies.

"It is I, Yvonne," said a voice.

"What is it? What has been happening?

"It was I. I set them against each other. They both loved one of the kitchen-maids. I made them jealous. I told Walt privily that she had favoured Dickon, and Dickon privily that she loved Walt. And now——"

She glanced at the shapeless heap, and shuddered. Agravaine nodded.

"No wedding-bells for her," he said, reverently.

"And I don't care. I did it to save you. But come! We are wasting time. Come! I will help you to escape."

A man who has been shut up for two days in a small room is seldom slow off the mark when a chance presents itself of taking exercise. Agravaine followed without a word, and together they crept down the dark staircase until they had reached the main hall. From somewhere in the distance came the rhythmic snores of scurvy knaves getting their eight hours.

Softly Yvonne unbolted a small door, and, passing through it, Agravaine found himself looking up at the stars, while the great walls of the castle towered above him.

"Good-bye," said Yvonne.

There was a pause. For the first time Agravaine found himself examining the exact position of

He was fortunate enough to get it.

He had composed himself for sleep that night, and was just dropping comfortably off, when from the other side of the door he heard the sound of angry voices.

It was enough to arouse him. On the previous night silence had reigned. Evidently something out of the ordinary was taking place.

He listened intently and distinguished words.

"Who was it I did see thee coming down the road with?"

"Who was it thou didst see me coming down the road with?"

"Aye, who was it I did see thee coming down the road with?"

"Who dost thou think thou art?"

"Who do I think that I am?"

"Aye, who dost thou think thou art?"

Agravaine could make nothing of it. As a matter of fact, he was hearing the first genuine cross-talk that had ever occurred in those dim, pre-music-hall days. In years to come dialogue on these lines was to be popular throughout the length and breadth of Great Britain. But till then it had been unknown.

The voices grew angrier. To an initiated listener it would have been plain that in a short while words would be found inadequate and the dagger, that medieval forerunner of the slap-stick, brought into play. But to Agravaine, all inexperienced, it came as a surprise when suddenly with a muffled thud two bodies fell against the door. There was a scuffling noise, some groans, and then silence.

His mind next turned to his immediate future. What were they going to do with him? On this point he felt tolerably comfortable. This imprisonment could mean nothing more than that he would be compelled to disgorge a ransom. This did not trouble him. He was rich, and, now that the situation had been switched to a purely business basis, he felt that he could handle it.

In any case, there was nothing to be gained by sitting up, so he went to bed, like a good philosopher.

The sun was pouring through the barred window when he was awoken by the entrance of a gigantic figure bearing food and drink.

He recognized him as one of the scurvy knaves who had dined at the bottom of the room the night before—a vast, beetle-browed fellow with a squint, a mop of red hair, and a genius for silence. To Agravaine's attempts to engage him in conversation he replied only with grunts, and in a short time left the room, closing and locking the door behind him.

He was succeeded at dusk by another of about the same size and ugliness, and with even less conversational *élan.* This one did not even grunt.

Small-talk, it seemed, was not an art cultivated in any great measure by the lower orders in the employment of Earl Dorm.

The next day passed without incident. In the morning the strabismic plug-ugly with the red hair brought him food and drink, while in the evening the non-grunter did the honours. It was a peaceful life, but tending towards monotony, and Agravaine was soon in the frame of mind which welcomes any break in the daily round.

"Can't what?"

"I can't."

His grip on her wrist tightened. From the other side of the door came the muffled sound of blows on the solid oak.

"Oh?" said Earl Dorm. "You can't, eh? Well, listen to me. You've got to. Do you understand? I admit he might be better-looking, but——"

"Father, I love him."

He released her wrist, and stared at her in the uncertain light.

"You love him!"

"Yes."

"Then what—? Why—? Well, I never did understand women," he said at last, and stumped off down the passage.

While this cryptic conversation was in progress, Agravaine, his worst apprehensions realized, was trying to batter down the door. After a few moments, however, he realized the futility of his efforts, and sat down on the bed to think.

At the risk of forfeiting the reader's respect, it must be admitted that his first emotion was one of profound relief. If he was locked up like this, it must mean that that dragon story was fictitious, and that all danger was at an end of having to pit his inexperience against a ravening monster who had spent a lifetime devouring knights. He had never liked the prospect, though he had been prepared to go through with it, and to feel that it was definitely cancelled made up for a good deal.

white-faced young lady had plunged in upon you and urged you to immediate flight, wouldn't that jar you?

It jarred Agravaine.

"Eh?" he cried.

"Fly! Fly, Sir Knight."

Another footstep sounded in the passage. The damsel gave a startled look over her shoulder.

"And what's all this?"

Earl Dorm appeared in the dim-lit corridor. His voice had a nasty tinkle in it.

"Your—your daughter," said Agravaine, hurriedly, "was just telling me that breakfast would——"

The sentence remained unfinished. A sudden movement of the earl's hand, and the great door banged in his face. There came the sound of a bolt shooting into its socket. A key turned in the lock. He was trapped.

Outside, the earl had seized his daughter by the wrist and was administering a paternal cross-examination.

"What were you saying to him?"

Yvonne did not flinch.

"I was bidding him fly."

"If he wants to leave this castle," said the earl, grimly, "he'll have to."

"Father," said Yvonne, "I can't."

and armour. At the time it had seemed to him that the Earl's remark that the latter needed polishing and the former stropping betrayed only a kindly consideration for his guest's well-being. Now, it had the aspect of being part of a carefully-constructed plot.

On the other hand—here philosophy came to his rescue—if anybody did mean to start anything, his sword and armour might just as well not be there. Any one of those mammoth low-brows at the door could eat him, armour and all.

He resumed his meal, uneasy but resigned.

Dinner at Earl Dorm's was no lunch-counter scuffle. It started early and finished late. It was not till an advanced hour that Agravaine was conducted to his room.

The room which had been allotted to him was high up in the eastern tower. It was a nice room, but to one in Agravaine's state of suppressed suspicion a trifle too solidly upholstered. The door was of the thickest oak, studded with iron nails. Iron bars formed a neat pattern across the only window.

Hardly had Agravaine observed these things when the door opened, and before him stood the damsel Yvonne, pale of face and panting for breath.

She stumbled into the room and gulped.

"Fly!" she whispered.

Reader, if you had come to spend the night in the lonely castle of a perfect stranger with a shifty eye and a rogues' gallery smile, and on retiring to your room had found the door kick-proof and the window barred, and if, immediately after your discovery of these phenomena, a

this castle. A conviction began to steal over him that in some way he was being played with, that some game was afoot which he did not understand, that—in a word—there was dirty work at the cross-roads.

There was a touch of mystery in the atmosphere which made him vaguely uneasy. When a fiery dragon is ravaging the countryside to such an extent that the C.Q.D. call has been sent out to the Round Table, a knight has a right to expect the monster to be the main theme of conversation. The tendency on his host's part was apparently to avoid touching on the subject at all. He was vague and elusive; and the one topic on which an honest man is not vague and elusive is that of fiery dragons. It was not right. It was as if one should 'phone for the police and engage them, on arrival, in a discussion on the day's football results.

A wave of distrust swept over Agravaine. He had heard stories of robber chiefs who lured strangers into their strongholds and then held them prisoners while the public nervously dodged their anxious friends who had formed subscription lists to make up the ransom. Could this be such a case? The man certainly had an evasive manner and a smile which would have justified any jury in returning a verdict without leaving the box. On the other hand, there was Yvonne. His reason revolted against the idea of that sweet girl being a party to any such conspiracy.

No, probably it was only the Earl's unfortunate manner. Perhaps he suffered from some muscular weakness of the face which made him smile like that.

Nevertheless, he certainly wished that he had not allowed himself to be deprived of his sword

company to take their meals together. The guests sat at the upper table, the ladies in a gallery above them, while the usual drove of men-at-arms, archers, malapert rogues, varlets, scurvy knaves, scullions, and plug-uglies, attached to all medieval households, squashed in near the door, wherever they could find room.

The retinue of Earl Dorm was not strong numerically—the household being, to judge from appearances, one that had seen better days; but it struck Agravaine that what it lacked in numbers it made up in toughness. Among all those at the bottom of the room there was not one whom it would have been agreeable to meet alone in a dark alley. Of all those foreheads not one achieved a height of more than one point nought four inches. A sinister collection, indeed, and one which, Agravaine felt, should have been capable of handling without his assistance any dragon that ever came into the world to stimulate the asbestos industry.

He was roused from his reflections by the voice of his host.

"I hope you are not tired after your journey, Sir Agravaine? My little girl did not bore you, I trust? We are very quiet folk here. Country mice. But we must try to make your visit interesting."

Agravaine felt that the dragon might be counted upon to do that. He said as much.

"Ah yes, the dragon," said Earl Dorm, "I was forgetting the dragon. I want to have a long talk with you about that dragon. Not now. Later on."

His eye caught Agravaine's and he smiled that weak, cunning smile of his. And for the first time the knight was conscious of a curious feeling that all was not square and above-board in

would not even have the melancholy satisfaction of giving the creature indigestion. For all the impression he was likely to make on that vast interior, he might as well be a salted almond.

As they were speaking, a dim mass on the skyline began to take shape.

"Behold!" said the damsel. "My father's castle." And presently they were riding across the drawbridge and through the great gate, which shut behind them with a clang.

As they dismounted a man came out through a door at the further end of the courtyard.

"Father," said Yvonne, "this is the gallant knight Sir Agravaine, who has come to—" it seemed to Agravaine that she hesitated for a moment.

"To tackle our dragon?" said her father. "Excellent. Come right in."

Earl Dorm of the Hills was a small, elderly man, with what Agravaine considered a distinctly furtive air about him. His eyes were too close together, and he was over-lavish with a weak, cunning smile. Even Agravaine, who was in the mood to like the whole family, if possible, for Yvonne's sake, could not help feeling that appearances were against this particular exhibit. He might have a heart of gold beneath the outward aspect of a confidence-trick expert whose hobby was dog-stealing, but there was no doubt that his exterior did not inspire a genial glow of confidence.

"Very good of you to come," said the earl.

"It's a pleasure," said Agravaine. "I have been hearing all about the dragon."

"A great scourge," agreed his host. "We must have a long talk about it after dinner."

It was the custom in those days in the stately homes of England for the whole strength of the

up a magic prescription for him, rendering him immune to dragon-bites. But did dragons bite? Or did they whack at you with their tails? Or just blow fire?

There were a dozen such points that he would have liked to have settled before starting. It was silly to start out on a venture of this sort without special knowledge. He had half a mind to plead a forgotten engagement and go straight back.

Then he looked at the damsel, and his mind was made up. What did death matter if he could serve her?

He coughed. She came out of her reverie with a start.

"This dragon, now?" said Agravaine.

For a moment the damsel did not reply. "A fearsome worm, Sir Knight," she said at length. "It raveneth by day and by night. It breathes fire from its nostrils."

"Does it!" said Agravaine. "*Does* it! You couldn't give some idea what it looks like, what kind of *size* it is?"

"Its body is as thick as ten stout trees, and its head touches the clouds."

"Does it!" said Agravaine thoughtfully. "*Does* it!"

"Oh, Sir Knight, I pray you have a care."

"I will," said Agravaine. And he had seldom said anything more fervently. The future looked about as bad as it could be. Any hopes he may have entertained that this dragon might turn out to be comparatively small and inoffensive were dissipated. This was plainly no debilitated wreck of a dragon, its growth stunted by excessive fire-breathing. A body as thick as ten stout trees! He

The fact was that Sir Agravaine had fallen in love at first sight. The moment he had caught a glimpse of the damsel Yvonne, he loved her devotedly. To others she seemed plain and unattractive. To him she was a Queen of Beauty. He was amazed at the inexplicable attitude of the knights around him. He had expected them to rise in a body to clamour for the chance of assisting this radiant vision. He could hardly believe, even now, that he was positively the only starter.

"This is Sir Agravaine the Dolorous," said the king to the damsel. "Will you take him as your champion?"

Agravaine held his breath. But all was well. The damsel bowed.

"Then, Sir Agravaine," said the king, "perhaps you had better have your charger sent round at once. I imagine that the matter is pressing—time and—er—dragons wait for no man."

Ten minutes later Agravaine, still dazed, was jogging along to the hills, with the damsel perched behind him.

It was some time before either of them spoke. The damsel seemed preoccupied, and Agravaine's mind was a welter of confused thoughts, the most prominent of which and the one to which he kept returning being the startling reflection that he, who had pined for romance so long, had got it now in full measure.

A dragon! Fiery withal. Was he absolutely certain that he was capable of handling an argument with a fiery dragon? He would have given much for a little previous experience of this sort of thing. It was too late now, but he wished he had had the forethought to get Merlin to put

The king had recourse to the direct appeal. "Sir Gawain, this Court would be greatly indebted to you if——"

Sir Gawain said he had strained a muscle at the last tournament.

"Sir Pelleas."

The king's voice was growing flat with consternation. The situation was unprecedented.

Sir Pelleas said he had an ingrowing toe-nail.

The king's eye rolled in anguish around the table. Suddenly it stopped. It brightened. His look of dismay changed to one of relief.

A knight had risen to his feet. It was Agravaine.

"Ah!" said the king, drawing a deep breath.

Sir Agravaine gulped. He was feeling more nervous than he had ever felt in his life. Never before had he risen to volunteer his services in a matter of this kind, and his state of mind was that of a small boy about to recite his first piece of poetry.

It was not only the consciousness that every eye, except one of Sir Balin's which had been closed in the tournament that afternoon, was upon him. What made him feel like a mild gentleman in a post-office who has asked the lady assistant if she will have time to attend to him soon and has caught her eye, was the fact that he thought he had observed the damsel Yvonne frown as he rose. He groaned in spirit. This damsel, he felt, wanted the proper goods or none at all. She might not be able to get Sir Lancelot or Sir Galahad; but she was not going to be satisfied with a half-portion.

An awkward silence was broken by the king.

"Er—yes?" he said.

The damsel halted.

"Your majesty," she cried, "I am in distress. I crave help!"

"Just so," said the king, uneasily, flashing an apprehensive glance at the rows of perturbed faces before him. "Just *so*. What—er—what is the exact nature of the—ah—trouble? Any assistance these gallant knights can render will, I am sure, be—ah—eagerly rendered."

He looked imploringly at the silent warriors. As a rule, this speech was the signal for roars of applause. But now there was not even a murmur.

"I may say enthusiastically," he added.

Not a sound.

"Precisely," said the king, ever tactful. "And now—you were saying?"

"I am Yvonne, the daughter of Earl Dorm of the Hills," said the damsel, "and my father has sent me to ask protection from a gallant knight against a fiery dragon that ravages the countryside."

"A dragon, gentlemen," said the king, aside. It was usually a safe draw. Nothing pleased the knight of that time more than a brisk bout with a dragon. But now the tempting word was received in silence.

"Fiery," said the king.

Some more silence.

silent and moody. To the jests of Dragonet he turned a deaf ear. And when his neighbour, Sir Kay, arguing with Sir Percivale on current form, appealed to him to back up his statement that Sir Gawain, though a workman-like middle-weight, lacked the punch, he did not answer, though the subject was one on which he held strong views. He sat on, brooding.

As he sat there, a man-at-arms entered the hall.

"Your majesty," he cried, "a damsel in distress waits without."

There was a murmur of excitement and interest.

"Show her in," said the king, beaming.

The man-at-arms retired. Around the table the knights were struggling into an upright position in their seats and twirling their moustaches. Agravaine alone made no movement. He had been through this sort of thing so often. What were distressed damsels to him? His whole demeanour said, as plainly as if he had spoken the words, "What's the use?"

The crowd at the door parted, and through the opening came a figure at the sight of whom the expectant faces of the knights turned pale with consternation. For the new-comer was quite the plainest girl those stately halls had ever seen. Possibly the only plain girl they had ever seen, for no instance is recorded in our authorities of the existence at that period of any such.

The knights gazed at her blankly. Those were the grand old days of chivalry, when a thousand swords would leap from their scabbards to protect defenceless woman, if she were beautiful. The present seemed something in the nature of a special case, and nobody was quite certain as to the correct procedure.

is a place in the world for the strong, ugly man, and there is a place for the weak, handsome man. But to fall short both in features and in muscle is to stake your all on brain. And in the days of King Arthur you did not find the populace turning out to do homage to brain. It was a drug in the market. Agravaine was a good deal better equipped than his contemporaries with grey matter, but his height in his socks was but five feet four; and his muscles, though he had taken three correspondence courses in physical culture, remained distressingly flaccid. His eyes were pale and mild, his nose snub, and his chin receded sharply from his lower lip, as if Nature, designing him, had had to leave off in a hurry and finish the job anyhow. The upper teeth, protruding, completed the resemblance to a nervous rabbit.

Handicapped in this manner, it is no wonder that he should feel sad and lonely in King Arthur's court. At heart he ached for romance; but romance passed him by. The ladies of the court ignored his existence, while, as for those wandering damsels who came periodically to Camelot to complain of the behaviour of dragons, giants, and the like, and to ask permission of the king to take a knight back with them to fight their cause (just as, nowadays, one goes out and calls a policeman), he simply had no chance. The choice always fell on Lancelot or some other popular favourite.

The tournament was followed by a feast. In those brave days almost everything was followed by a feast. The scene was gay and animated. Fair ladies, brave knights, churls, varlets, squires, scurvy knaves, men-at-arms, malapert rogues—all were merry. All save Agravaine. He sat

"Score-cards: ye cannot tell the jousters without a score-card." All was revelry and excitement.

A hush fell on the throng. From either end of the arena a mounted knight in armour had entered.

The herald raised his hand.

"Ladeez'n gemmen! Battling Galahad and Agravaine the Dolorous. Galahad on my right, Agravaine on my left. Squires out of the ring. Time!"

A speculator among the crowd offered six to one on Galahad, but found no takers. Nor was the public's caution without reason.

A moment later the two had met in a cloud of dust, and Agravaine, shooting over his horse's crupper, had fallen with a metallic clang.

He picked himself up, and limped slowly from the arena. He was not unused to this sort of thing. Indeed, nothing else had happened to him in his whole jousting career.

The truth was that Sir Agravaine the Dolorous was out of his element at King Arthur's court, and he knew it. It was this knowledge that had given him that settled air of melancholy from which he derived his title.

Until I came upon this black-letter MS. I had been under the impression, like, I presume, everybody else, that every Knight of the Round Table was a model of physical strength and beauty. Malory says nothing to suggest the contrary. Nor does Tennyson. But apparently there were exceptions, of whom Sir Agravaine the Dolorous must have been the chief.

There was, it seems, nothing to mitigate this unfortunate man's physical deficiencies. There

SOME TIME AGO, when spending a delightful weekend at the ancestral castle of my dear old friend, the Duke of Weatherstonhope (pronounced Wop), I came across an old black-letter MS. It is on this that the story which follows is based.

I have found it necessary to touch the thing up a little here and there, for writers in those days were weak in construction. Their idea of telling a story was to take a long breath and start droning away without any stops or dialogue till the thing was over.

I have also condensed the title. In the original it ran, " 'How it came about that ye good Knight Sir Agravaine ye Dolorous of ye Table Round did fare forth to succor a damsel in distress and after divers journeyings and perils by flood and by field did win her for his bride and right happily did they twain live ever afterwards,' by Ambrose ye monk."

It was a pretty snappy title for those times, but we have such a high standard in titles nowadays that I have felt compelled to omit a few yards of it.

We may now proceed to the story.

The great tournament was in full swing. All through the afternoon boiler-plated knights on mettlesome chargers had hurled themselves on each other's spears, to the vast contentment of all. Bright eyes shone; handkerchiefs fluttered; musical voices urged chosen champions to knock the cover off their brawny adversaries. The cheap seats had long since become hoarse with emotion. All round the arena rose the cries of itinerant merchants: "Iced malvoisie,"

SIR AGRAVAINE

This edition first published in the U.K. 1984 by Blandford Press,
Link House, West Street, Poole, Dorset, BH15 1LL

Sir Agravaine by P. G. Wodehouse first published by Methuen & Co.,
1914 as part of the volume *The Man Upstairs*
COPYRIGHT ALL RIGHTS RESERVED
Illustrations © 1984 Rodger McPhail

Permission to reproduce *Sir Agravaine* is given by the
Hutchinson Publishing Group Ltd., 17–21 Conway St., London, W.1.,
who now publish *The Man Upstairs and Other Stories* by
P. G. Wodehouse

British Library Cataloguing in Publication Data

Wodehouse, P. G.
    Sir Agravaine
    I. Title   II. McPhail, Rodger
    823'.912[F]   PR6045.053

        ISBN 0 7137 1510 3

Typeset by MS Filmsetting Limited, Frome, Somerset
Printed in Spain by Graficromo SA, Cordoba

SIR AGRAVAINE

P. G. WODEHOUSE

Illustrated by Rodger McPhail

BLANDFORD PRESS
POOLE · DORSET

SIR AGRAVAINE

WITHDRAWN